FIVE LITTLE DUCKS

SCHOLASTIC INC.
New York Toronto London Auckland Sydney

Five Little Ducks

AN OLD RHYME · ILLUSTRATED BY

Pamela Paparone

ISBN 0-590-96581-6

Illustrations copyright © 1995 by Pamela Paparone.
All rights reserved. Published by Scholastic Inc., 555 Broadway, New York, NY 10012,
by arrangement with North-South Books Inc.

12 11 10 9 8 7 6 5   7 8 9/9 0 1 2/0

Printed in the U.S.A.   14

First Scholastic printing, January 1997

The artwork was created with acrylic paint and colored pencil.
Designed by Marc Cheshire.

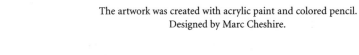

To J.O. with love

Five little ducks went out one day,
Over the hills and far away.

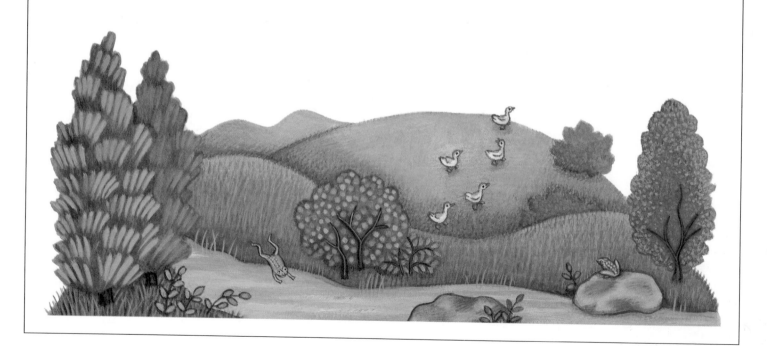

Mother duck said,

"Quack, quack, quack, quack."

But only four little ducks came back.

Four little ducks went out one day,
Over the hills and far away.

Mother duck said,

"Quack, quack, quack, quack."

But only three little ducks came back.

Three little ducks went out one day,
Over the hills and far away.

Mother duck said,

"Quack, quack, quack, quack."

But only two little ducks came back.

Two little ducks went out one day,
Over the hills and far away.

Mother duck said,

"Quack, quack, quack, quack."

But only one little duck came back.

One little duck went out one day,
Over the hills and far away.

Mother duck said,

"Quack, quack, quack, quack."

But none of the little ducks came back.

Sad mother duck went out one day,
Over the hills and far away.

Mother duck said,
"Quack, quack, quack, quack."

And all of her five little ducks came back!